PIPPBROOK BOOKS

First published in the UK in 1999 by Templar Publishing
This softback edition produced in the UK in 2015 by Pippbrook Books,
an imprint of Templar Publishing,
part of the Bonnier Publishing Group,
The Plaza, 535 King's Road, London, SW10 0SZ
www.templarco.co.uk
www.bonnierpublishing.com

1 3 5 7 9 10 8 6 4 2

ISBN 978-1-78370-558-0

Designed by Hayley Bebb and Manhar Chauhan
Edited by Dugald Steer and Liza Miller

Printed in Malaysia

PIPPBROOK
BOOKS

LITTLE LAMB
to the rescue

Written by Erica Briers ✳ Illustrated by Stephanie Boey

It was spring, and out in the green fields,
Little Lamb was struggling to her feet. This was her first day
in the world and she was very excited to be alive.

She stood up on her wobbly legs and looked around her.

All the lambs in the field were different – some were black, some were white, and some were a mixture. Little Lamb was mostly white, but she had lovely black ears, a black nose and black feet so it looked like she was wearing socks!

The lambs were different sizes too, and Little Lamb was the littlest of all. But she had a big heart, and wanted more than anything to be useful. She decided to set off around the farm to see what she could do.

That day, the sheep were being rounded up ready to have their woolly coats sheared.

"Please can I come too?" asked Little Lamb.

"Not yet," said her father, the big curly-horned ram. "You are still far too small to be sheared, you don't have enough wool. Run along and play, Little Lamb."

So Little Lamb went to see the big Shire horse, who was about to take the farmer to market in the farm cart.

"Please can I help?" asked Little Lamb.

"Oh no," snorted the horse. "You are far too little to pull this great big cart."

So Little Lamb went to see the chickens. The farm dog was there, watching over the newly hatched chicks just in case the fox came prowling around.

"Please can I help?" asked Little Lamb.

But the farm dog just said kindly, "You are so tiny, I think the fox might eat you as well as the chicks!"

"Little Lamb, Little Lamb!" cried the farm ducklings as she walked past the pond. "You're far too small to help anyone at all!"

And the cheeky little ducklings waddled along after her, laughing and quacking until poor Little Lamb ran away into the meadow.

Poor Little Lamb! She sat down in the daisy patch, feeling miserable and unwanted.

Then, among the buzzing bees, she heard a faint cheeping noise. Little Lamb followed the sound to the base of a shady tree. Trembling in the long grass there was a fluffy baby bird.

"Please can you help me?" cheeped the baby bird. "I have fallen from my nest in the tree, and I'm worried that the fox might find me soon!"

"I'm afraid not," said Little Lamb, "for I'm too small to help anyone at all!"

But the baby bird cheeped so sadly that Little Lamb knew she had to do something.

So Little Lamb leaned right down to the ground, and the baby bird hopped right onto her head.
Then Little Lamb carefully put her front feet on the fence and stretched higher and higher until...

... the baby bird hopped right back into his nest.

The baby bird was very happy to be back with his brothers and sisters. And the baby bird's mother was very pleased to have him safely back home.

"Thank you, Little Lamb," she said. "You are the kindest, most helpful animal on this farm. We hope you will always be around to help us!"

And all the baby birds chirped noisily in agreement.